Butter,
the Lost Kitten

Patricia Simmons Taylor

Illustrated by
Nada Serafimovic & Bojan Bergamo-Ravlic

Butter,
the Lost Kitten

Patricia Simmons Taylor
Illustrated by
Nada Serafimovic & Bojan Bergamo-Ravlic

ISBN-13: 978-1975925871

ISBN-10: 1975925874

Edited by Patricia Simmons Taylor and Diane Simmons Dill.
Facebook: https://www.facebook.com/RightwriteProductions

Formatting and Interior Design by Diane Simmons Dill.

Cover design by Nada Serafimovic and Diane Simmons Dill.

Artwork by Nada Serafimovic and Bojan Bergamo-Ravlic.
https://www.fiverr.com/nadaserafimovic and
https://www.fiverr.com/bojanbergamo.

PRINTED IN THE UNITED STATES OF AMERICA

Dedication

This book is dedicated to my two wonderful grandchildren. I'm so grateful to have you in my life, and I love you with all my heart.

Why I Wrote This Book

I was able to rescue a tiny yellow kitten many years ago and he was the inspiration for this book. I believe God expects us to help animals as well as people and is pleased when we do so.

R.I.P. little Peanut—you were a loving, almost human pet who came into my life at a time when we needed each other. I will never forget you!

Patricia S. Taylor
September 2017

The righteous care for the
needs of their animals.
~Proverbs 12:10 (NIV)

Olivia was awakened one summer morning by the sun shining through her bedroom window. She rubbed her eyes and felt like today was going to be a wonderful day!
She smelled bacon frying and knew it would taste delicious!

Olivia sat down at the kitchen table to eat breakfast.
Her mom smiled and said, "Good morning!" Olivia gave her mom a hug.
They bowed their heads as her mom thanked God for their food.

Olivia and her mom laughed, talked, and enjoyed their wonderful meal.
Olivia helped clear the table when they finished eating and went
to her room to get dressed.

Olivia went to the back door to go outside and play.
She stopped when she heard a tiny scratching and crying sound.
She called her Mom and they opened the door. She couldn't
believe her eyes! A tiny yellow kitten stood there, meowing
and trembling in fear.

Olivia's mom got a big fluffy towel to wrap the kitten in. Olivia asked, "Oh Mom, can I keep him?" Her Mom smiled and thought for a moment. "Yes," she finally said. "I suppose you have found a new friend." Olivia was overjoyed!

They drove to a pet store nearby and bought some supplies. Olivia had a big smile on her face as they drove back home. She couldn't wait for her best friend, Tori, to get home from her family's vacation to the beach. She knew that Tori would love her little kitten, too.

The kitten was awake and meowing loudly as if to say, "I'm hungry!" He ate quickly and drank some water. Then he washed his face with his paws. Olivia's mom asked her what she was going to name her kitten. Olivia said, "Well, he *is* yellow so I think I'll name him Butter!" This made her Mom smile. Butter meowed and almost seemed to smile, too!

Olivia's mom said, "I will call the vet's office and make an appointment to get Butter checked out as soon as possible." This made Olivia feel good because she wanted Butter to be healthy.

When morning came, Olivia got up early. She was almost too excited to eat breakfast! They left to go to the vet's office with Olivia holding Butter in his box on her lap.

The vet checked him over and said he was a healthy cat! The vet's assistant gave Butter a warm bath. Holding Butter on the way home, Olivia knew it was going to be a great day!

Olivia's mom heard her laughter from the next room and went in to watch them play. She knew she had made the right decision to allow Olivia to keep the homeless kitten. She was already falling in love with him herself!

A few days later Olivia awoke to Butter gently pawing her hand as if to say, "Wake up! I'm hungry and I want to play!"

Olivia's eyes popped open even wider! She smelled coffee and bacon and thought, "Dad's home!"

Her Dad came into the bedroom and scooped her and Butter up in his arms. She was so happy to have her Dad back home! Butter meowed at him and he laughed. He carried both of them into the kitchen for breakfast.

Olivia fed Butter and sat down with her parents to eat. Her Dad said he was happy that she had Butter for a pet and knew she would take good care of him.

Olivia offered to ask the blessing over their food. She thanked God, not only for their food, but for her dad's safe return and, of course, for her new kitten, Butter!

Olivia got permission from her mom to call her friend Tori to tell her all about Butter and asked if Tori could come over tomorrow. Her mom smiled and said, "Of course." Olivia left her Mom and Dad talking at the table and and went into her room to get dressed. She played with Butter and made the call to Tori.

Tori was excited too! She and Olivia made plans for Tori to come over at 9:00 o'clock the next morning. Olivia was so happy that she and Tori could have fun playing with Butter!

Olivia held Butter close and spoke to him softly. "Oh, Butter! I am so glad that God let you find your way to my house so you could be my new friend." Butter curled up next to Olivia and went to sleep.

The next morning, Tori knocked on the door at 9:00 o'clock. She was already smiling when Olivia opened the door. "Oh, Butter is so cute!" she said. "I had fun at the beach, but I think you had more fun with Butter," she added.

Tori snuggled Butter close. Then she and Olivia had so much fun playing with him and giggling at his funny movements. "He can run so fast!" Olivia said.

Tori had to go home, and Olivia spent the rest of the day playing with Butter and taking care of him.

Soon, it was time for Olivia to go to bed. She went to sleep dreaming about all the adventures that she and Butter would have.

One thing Olivia knew for sure was that Butter was no longer lost! He had found a good home. Yes, it was certainly going to be a great summer!

The End

Acknowledgement

I thank God for His love and mercy and for the salvation Jesus provided to me. There have been many times during my lifetime when the Lord rescued me and gave me refuge and hope. I am so grateful for His amazing grace and unending love.

My two wonderful sons have been there for me always. Even during the deaths of their brother many years ago and their father in August 2016, they never wavered in their support and encouragement. My husband would be so happy to see this book because he encouraged me so much over the years.

To my precious grandson and granddaughter, thank you for always showing me love and appreciation. You are always in my corner no matter what endeavor I undertake. You are shining lights in my life, and I love you with all of my heart.

To my sister, Diane Simmons Dill, thank you for all that you have done to help me publish this book. From the editing to the formatting to obtaining the artwork, you worked tirelessly to help make my book a reality. You have never failed to encourage me in life and in writing. You are a blessing to me.

To Nada Serafimovic and Bojan Bergamo-Ravlic, who illustrated my book, thank you for all your hard work and for the beautiful artwork in my book. Your images brought the story to life. Thank you both so much.

A Message From the Author

Thank you for reading my book! My prayer is for everyone to love animals and care for them, especially those who are lost, afraid, or unloved.

May I ask a favor of you? If you and your child enjoyed the book, would you please take just a moment to leave a review on Amazon.com? It would mean so much to me.

Thank you, and may God bless you!

Patricia

Hey, kids! If you enjoyed the storybook version, I hope you will check out the e-book and coloring book versions on Amazon.com! The e-book will enable you to read the story on-the-go, and the coloring book will allow you to color the images with the colors you choose. You can show your own special creativity while reading a lovely story!

About the Author

Patricia Simmons Taylor is an Alabama native who has been writing since grade school. She loves to write on a variety of topics, such as fiction, nonfiction, poetry, quotes and other inspirational writings. She has used her writing on bookmarks, shirts, tote bags, coffee mugs, and notecards. She is quick to give God the credit for her gift of writing and for anything she has accomplished in life.

She is the mother of three sons, one of whom, Jeff, went home to Heaven in 1983. Her husband, A.L., followed him in 2016. Her two sons live nearby, and her two beautiful grandchildren light up her life.

She is the also the author of *Sweet Morning Glory*, a book of poetry and other inspirational writings. Patricia is currently working on her third book, *The Grace of a Sparrow,* which is a book about her eldest son's life, head injury, recovery, and death. She details her family's journey with intense, devastating grief while never giving up and totally trusting the Lord's perfect will for their lives. Though based on a sad personal story, it is a book about hope, meant to offer encouragement to other grieving parents and families.

Patricia enjoys traveling and spending time with her friends and family, especially with her grandchildren. A long-time member of Unity Baptist Church, Patricia lives in the Birmingham, Alabama area with her sweet and spoiled cat, Domino.

To contact Patricia for speaking engagements or to find out more about her books, she is available via email at booseca1@bellsouth.net.

Books by Patricia Simmons Taylor

Butter, the Lost Kitten, and *Sweet Morning Glory* are available on Amazon in print and ebook formats.

Coming Soon: *The Grace of a Sparrow*

Made in United States
Orlando, FL
26 August 2023

36438937R00020